WHITE CHOCOLATE AND WORRIES

CANDY COVERED COZY MYSTERIES, BOOK 2

PATTI BENNING

SUMMER PRESCOTT BOOKS PUBLISHING

CHAPTER 1

CANDICE ROTHBURG LOOPED the scarf around her neck twice and pulled the knitted hat down tighter over her ears. She was well and truly sick of winter, but there was no avoiding the nasty weather. All she could do was hide from it under layers of warm clothes.

"You ready?" Eli, her husband, asked. He was wearing boots and a coat, but had foregone a scarf, gloves, and a hat, and Candice couldn't help but wonder for a moment if the man she had married was insane.

"I've just got to find my mittens," she said.

"Did you check your coat pockets?"

She did, and found them. Shooting him a grateful look, she pulled them on. Maybe he wasn't insane, after all. Maybe spending years working around ice cream had simply desensitized him to the cold.

"Thanks," she said. "I'm ready now. Let's get going, I don't want to be late for dinner."

They ventured outside, Eli pausing to lock the door behind them as Candice made her way to the car, which was already running. She got into the passenger side and settled down in the heated seat, closing the door firmly against the cold. The temperature outside was in the single digits, and she was sure she could feel her eyeballs freezing if she didn't blink enough.

"Only a few more months of this," Eli said as he got into the driver's seat, looking over at her huddled form.

"I might turn into an icicle before then."

"I'll stick you in front of the fireplace if that happens," he said, grinning at her.

"I'll melt all over the floor."

Their joking continued as Eli drove into Lake

Marion. Many of the Christmas decorations had been taken down, but a few houses still had them up, and the lights managed to cheer Candice up a bit. Christmas was the best part of winter, as far as she was concerned. Everything after was just cold and dreary until spring. It had been more fun back when she was a kid, with sledding and snow days to look forward to.

The nursing home, at least, still had its decorations up. It looked cheery and welcoming, and Candice gladly hurried up to the front doors once Eli had parked. The entrance had two sets of doors, and she punched in the code to the interior set as soon as the outer doors had shut. With a beep, the light on the keypad turned green, and she and Eli let themselves inside.

The interior was just as welcoming as the outside of the building had been. It smelled like food; cooking meat and something sweet and aromatic, probably whatever was for dessert. Homemade Christmas decorations lined the walls, and the artificial Christmas tree was still up in the common area, right next to the large fish tank. Candice walked over to look at the fish and, as she always did, wondered how much work it would be to maintain a tank of her own. She'd had a few goldfish when she was younger, but nothing this complicated, and they had never fared very well. Felix was the first pet she had truly been responsible for as an adult, and the idea of branching out was tempting.

A low conversation interrupted her fishy thoughts, and she straightened up to see a hugely tall and muscular man who looked like he was about a decade older than Candice walking down the hall with an elderly man she didn't recognize. They seemed to be having an argument of some sort.

"I'm not talking about it anymore, Morgan," the elderly man said in a mild but firm tone. "Let it drop, please. After all these years, it hardly matters anymore."

"It matters to me," the man, Morgan, answered with a huff. "I'd say I'm glad you haven't changed after all these years, Rudy, but I'm not. I'll be seeing you later." With that, he turned and headed toward the door. Candice watched him go, wondering what that had been about.

"There you are," a familiar voice said from behind her, and she turned to see Reggie, Eli's grandfather, approaching from the dining area. His grandson greeted him with a quick hug, and Candice straightened up to give him a hug of her own.

"It smells great in here," Eli said. "What's on the menu tonight?"

"Pork chops, mashed sweet potatoes, salad, and the chef's homemade rolls," Reggie said. "There's pie for dessert. I've got my eye on a table already, but we'd better hurry before someone else takes it. Empty tables go fast; we've got to snatch one up while we can."

They hurried — well, hurried as quickly as Reggie's stiff joints would allow — into the dining area, where Reggie led them to a round table with four seats in the corner. They took their seats and Candice sipped the glass of water that was waiting for her. She hadn't realized how hungry she was until she had smelled the delicious scent of cooking food. The water didn't do much to help, but at least it was something in her stomach. *Chocolate does not make a good lunch*, she told herself. She should have accepted Suri's offer to grab her a wrap when she went out for food earlier that day.

"Sorry we couldn't make it last week," Eli said. "I felt bad canceling, but David needed my help figuring out why the bottling machine at the brewery wasn't working, and Candice had to stay late to finish organizing her files for when she goes to visit the tax preparer and—"

"Don't worry about it," Reggie said, looking amused. "I'm not going to wither away just because you missed a visit. I'm glad to have you now, though."

"We're glad to be here," Candice said with a smile. She was about to ask him how his week had been, but was interrupted before she could begin by another resident's approach; he was the one she had seen in the hall earlier, who she didn't recognize.

"Can I join you?" he asked, gesturing at the empty chair.

"Make yourself at home, Rudy," Reggie said. "Let me introduce you to my grandson, Eli, and his wife, Candice. This is Rudolph Granger, one of our newest inmates." He winked at them as he spoke, and Candice knew he was joking. The nursing home was one of the nicer ones she'd seen, and hardly felt prison-like.

"It's nice to meet you," Candice said, smiling at him as he took a seat. Eli said something similar, and shook his hand.

"Thank you for letting me join you," Rudolph said. "I'm sorry if I'm interrupting a family meal, but your table was the only one with one seat left."

Candice shared a confused glance with her husband, but Reggie chuckled knowingly. "You're still avoiding her, then?"

Rudolph grimaced. "I don't have much choice. She won't leave me be unless I go out of my way to make it clear I don't want to talk to her."

"Rudy here has a little problem with an ex-sweetheart," Reggie explained. "They had a fling years ago, but it seems she never got over him."

"The feeling is not mutual," Rudolph muttered. "Lainey is nothing if not persistent. It's served her well over the years, I won't deny that, but someone our age should have learned when to take no for an answer by now."

"She'll figure it out eventually, and then some other poor soul will have to deal with her," Reggie said bracingly. "Maybe your daughter can come and give her a piece of her mind again."

"She's supposed to be here soon. I'll have to ask her to do just that."

A staff member approached carrying a laden tray and passed plates out to each of them. They dug in, and the next few minutes were consumed with silence. The food was a bit blander than what Candice was used to, since many of the residents had to watch their sodium intake, but it was still good.

"Oh, I almost forgot," Eli said suddenly, pausing as he raised a forkful of mashed sweet potatoes to his mouth. "Have you notified the director that you're going to be gone on Friday?"

"Yes, yes," Reggie said, waving a hand dismissively. "All the forms have been filled out and they're making a packet for my medications. All you'll have to do Friday morning is sign me out. It makes me feel a bit like a library book."

"Library books don't get to go ice fishing," Eli said.

Candice snorted. "I wouldn't be too sure about that. I might just sneak one out onto the lake."

"You can't read while you're fishing, Candice," Eli said, looking at her as if she had just stabbed him with her knife.

"I most certainly can, especially since it's *ice* fishing, and nothing happens most of the time anyway," she retorted. "You've already convinced me to go sit in a freezing tent for a few hours; don't tell me you're going to try to get me to actually pay attention to your sports radio too."

"It's tradition," Eli said.

"Then I'll make my own tradition of reading while you two listen to your sports show and we wait for nothing to nibble at our hooks."

"We'll get a bite this year," Eli said loyally.

Candice rolled her eyes good naturedly. "That's what you said last year. I'll believe it when I see it."

Their meal was interrupted halfway through by a harried looking woman who made a beeline for Rudolph once she spotted him. He half rose out of his chair to welcome her.

"This is my daughter, Emmy Baumer. And now that she's finally here, I'm going to have to excuse myself to dine privately with her. I'll see all of you fine people later, I'm sure."

His daughter, who looked to be maybe a decade older than Candice, tried to make excuses for her lateness, but he waved them away. He just looked glad to see her, and Candice smiled as she watched them go.

CHAPTER 2

THE WEEK PASSED QUICKLY. It had been easy to settle back into her normal routine after Christmas, so easy that life was almost boring. She woke up, ate breakfast and spent some time relaxing or cleaning the house before leaving for work, where she would spend the next few hours working alongside Allison, Logan, or Suri before going back home, eating dinner, spending time with Eli, and then going to bed just to wake up and do it all over again the next day.

It wasn't that she didn't like her life. She did. There was nowhere she would rather work than at Candice's Candies — her very own store that she had rebuilt practically from the ground up after the fire that had razed the building — and there was no one she would rather spend time with than Eli. She loved their farmhouse and their quiet evenings together.

But the way the days all seemed to blend together after a little while was disconcerting. She needed to find some sort of group to join, or maybe find a hobby to do on her own. As she bagged up yet another customer's purchase at the candy shop's register, her mind drifted back to the nursing home's fish tank. Maybe that would make a good hobby for her. It would at least take some time and research to set up, and it would add a nice ambiance to the house.

She knew she should be grateful that things were calmer now than they had been over the past few years. And she was. She would never want to go back to those long hours of driving Eli to and from physical therapy as he recovered from injuries that had almost taken his life, or agonizing over how she was going to afford to repair the candy shop. Things were better now. They were just also a little bit boring.

"Candice?" A pause. "Candice?"

She jerked her head up as she realized that Allison had been calling her name. "Sorry, what?"

"I was trying to let you know we're almost out of the caramel filled chocolate bars," her half-sister said, looking amused. "I was beginning to worry you'd gone deaf."

"My head was in the clouds," Candice admitted, feeling embarrassed and glad that Allison hadn't been a customer. "I'll put them on the list, thanks. We'll have more by tomorrow."

"We'd better, they're my favorite," the other woman said with a grin. "What were you daydreaming about?"

Candice glanced around to make sure that the store was empty, then leaned against the register with a sigh. "Fish."

"Fish?"

"Well, fish tanks. I was thinking of maybe getting one. It would give me something to do other than work. I never knew being an adult could be so... boring."

"I don't know anyone who would call your life boring," Allison said, looking amused.

"It feels like I've been repeating the same day over and over again since Christmas," she admitted. "It's all just snow, cold, work, sleep, repeat. There's the occasional nice dinner or visit with my family or fun evening in with Eli, but most of it is just so repetitive. It's driving me insane."

"You need something to break you from the doldrums," her friend agreed. "I'm not sure a fish tank is the most exciting way to do it, but to each their own, I guess."

"A fish tank probably isn't the most exciting thing," Candice admitted. "I just don't know what else I really like. It's weird. I've already got the candy shop, and Eli, and a great family — including you, of course — and a house. I should be happy, but I just feel like there's nothing to work toward anymore. Will I just do the same thing every day until I retire and pass the store on to someone else?"

"Jeez, I didn't know you'd be having an existential crisis today," Allison said. She pulled up one of the stools behind the counter and sat down. "All right, let's talk. Just so you know, my therapy rate is triple my normal rate."

"Yeah, yeah. I'll pay you in chocolate."

"Good." Her friend's eyes twinkled, but then she became more serious. "Well, you're not even thirty yet and you've already got your life pretty much figured out. And that's a good thing, of course, but for the past few years you've been working constantly toward something — first college, then opening your own business, then the house, then everything that happened with Eli, then reopening the business... Let's just put it mildly and say you've been insanely busy. It makes sense that the calm after the storm would feel weird. Are you really that unhappy?"

"No," Candice said. "I wouldn't say I'm unhappy at all. Moment to moment, things are great. I'm happy working here. I'm happy with Eli. It's just when I look at the big picture... I don't know, it feels like I'm just killing time. There should be something... more."

It wasn't the clearest explanation, but her friend

seemed to understand what she meant. "Are you thinking about having kids?"

Candice blanched. "No. Goodness, no. Not yet. Not for years. I'm so not ready for that."

"Do you want to travel or something?"

"Traveling would be nice," she said, taking a moment to think about it. "It would definitely be fun. But I guess I want something with more purpose."

"Like a fish tank," Allison said, her voice deadpan but her eyes amused.

"Very funny," Candice said, making a face at her friend.

"Well, you're the one who—" Allison broke off mid-sentence, her eyes narrowing as she looked toward the door. "Heads up. I'll let you deal with this."

Candice turned around and saw a familiar, but unwelcome, face. Old Mr. Smith, her worst customer. She bit back a groan. Allison was already on her way through the door to the back, and Candice glared at her retreating form. Some friend.

She made sure she had a bright, cheery smile on her face by the time he opened the door and made his way inside. She braced herself for his usual criticism, but he surprised her by ignoring her completely. He moved past the register and walked directly to the shelf where the ginger hard candies he liked were kept. Once he had selected his usual handful, he came over to the register, not even looking at the rows and rows of other candy. He hadn't even glanced at the small section of candy that contained artificial sweetener — a new addition that she was sure he would love to hate.

In months past, Mr. Smith had seemed to enjoy nothing more than telling her that she was selling poison that rotted the teeth out of America's youth, and a few other choice phrases that she always did her best to ignore. She had never seen him so subdued, and her annoyance quickly turned into worry. She might not particularly like the man, but that didn't mean she wished him ill.

"Is this all?" she asked as he put the candy on the counter. He nodded once, then dug into his pocket for his wallet. She rang his order up and put the candies into a small paper bag for him. She took his offered payment, but before handing the bag over, she just had to ask. "Is everything all right, Mr. Smith?"

"I'm terribly worried about a friend of mine," he admitted. He met her eyes. "Thank you for asking."

He seemed to mean it, and Candice once again found herself feeling guilty about her less-than-kind thoughts toward the man. "I'm so sorry," she said. "Is he sick? I could put together a 'Get Well Soon' package for you."

Mr. Smith shook his head. "He's missing."

"Oh." Candice mentally kicked herself. "I'm so sorry."

"I blame the young people who work at that nursing home," Mr. Smith said, sounding more like the man she had grown to know. "They're all too busy looking at their phones to pay attention to their jobs. He probably just walked out, right under their incompetent noses. I'm sure it took them hours to even notice he was gone."

"Wait, someone's missing from the nursing home?" Candice asked, her eyes going wide as her thoughts went to Reggie. Of course, she and Eli would have heard if he was missing, but she couldn't help the flare of worry she felt.

"It's been on the news," he said, giving her a haughty sniff as he grabbed the bag of candy from her. "This proves my point. Young people today don't even notice what's right in front of their faces." He shot a glare at the TV hanging in the corner, on which the local news was playing silently, then turned and left the store in a huff.

CHAPTER 3

As soon as Mr. Smith left, Candice pulled out her phone and searched *Missing Person Lake Marion.* Most of the links were years old, but the top two were recent. She clicked on one and read the article, feeling her stomach clench with worry.

Mr. Smith had been telling the truth, not that she had doubted it. There was a person missing from the nursing home, and worse, it was a name she recognized. Rudolph Granger. She had eaten dinner with him not even a week ago. He had been missing since Wednesday. Two days. How could she not have heard about this?

She glanced toward the TV guiltily. Sure, it was turned onto the news, but it had been silent all day since they had the radio playing instead. And she and Eli didn't have cable at home; they simply watched all of their shows through streaming services. While her phone kept her updated on major national and international news, it seemed that the local news had somehow slipped through the cracks.

All of her existential thoughts forgotten, she started a text message to Eli, telling him what had happened and asking him to check in on Reggie. Not that he needed her to ask; she knew he would do it anyway. Eli always seemed to know what to do for others.

That done, she put her phone away and tried to turn her focus back to work, but it was difficult. She couldn't stop thinking of Rudolph. He had been so nice during dinner, and so vibrant and alive even if he was in a nursing home. It was hard to think of what might have happened to him. She wondered if he had snuck out of his own volition, perhaps to get away from that scorned lover of his. She could almost see that, and it was tempting to believe, but she knew there was likely more to the story.

The rest of the day passed with agonizing slowness, and it was with relief that Candice pulled into her driveway that evening. She had gotten a text back from Eli saying that he was going to head over to the nursing home and see what was going on, but she hadn't heard anything past that. His car was in the driveway, which meant she would finally be able to hear what had really happened.

The house was warm and smelled like roasting beef, a scent that made Candice's mouth water. Unlike her mother, who spent all day around foods like soups, sandwiches, and cold cut meat, Candice spent most of her time around candy. That meant that unless she wanted to stuff herself full of sweets, she usually went home hungry. Today, however, even the promise of a pot roast couldn't distract her from her thoughts about the missing man. She let herself into the house and took off her outerwear before finding Eli in the kitchen. He was adding the last touches to the roast in the slow cooker.

"Hey," she said as she entered the room. "It smells great in here."

"I'm glad," he said. "I wasn't quite sure how it would turn out. I stopped at the store after visiting Reggie and saw the roast on sale. I couldn't resist."

"How did that go?" she asked, taking advantage of the easy segue into what she really wanted to talk about. "Did Reggie know anything about what actually happened?"

"No," Eli said, frowning as he prodded the roast with a fork. "He didn't seem to know anything that wasn't already reported on the news. He told me that Rudolph was at dinner Wednesday night, then Thursday morning, he never came to breakfast. He told me he remembered hearing people rushing around the nursing home late Wednesday night, but he didn't know what they were doing until the announcement was made at breakfast the next day. According to him, Rudolph just up and vanished. He said he wasn't acting oddly at dinner or anything."

"Did you talk to anyone else at the nursing home about it?"

"I asked one of the staff members, but they didn't say much. I get the feeling they were told to keep quiet until they find him, so as not to risk saying anything that might get the nursing home in trouble."

"I hope they find him soon," Candice said. "Mr. Smith was really worried about him."

Eli raised his eyebrows as he looked at her. "I'm still shocked that you're actually getting along with him well enough to actually hold a conversation."

"It's surprisingly easy to get along with someone who isn't trying to blame your business for all the woes of the world. As terrible as it is to say, I like him better like this than how he normally is."

"At least it shows that he has a heart," Eli said. He turned back to the slow cooker and began cutting the pot roast. "This is done. Do you want to grab a couple of plates?"

"Sure," Candice said, straightening up from where she had been leaning on the counter. She still wasn't sure what to think of Mr. Smith, but those thoughts could wait. Right now, dinner called.

They ate in the living room, watching the newest episode of one of their favorite shows. Once dinner was over, Candice helped Eli clean up the kitchen, then they retreated to the living room for another hour or two until bed. They settled in for the night earlier than usual, since they had to wake up early the next morning. Candice would be lying if she said she was looking forward to ice fishing, but she was looking forward to seeing Reggie and getting out of the house. Maybe it wouldn't be all bad. She had a book to read, after all, and they would be bringing hot coffee and snacks. If they were lucky, they might even catch a fish.

CHAPTER 4

THEY GOT UP BEFORE DAWN. Without even a hint of light in the sky, it felt more like the middle of the night than the early hours of the morning. Despite the cup of coffee Candice had downed before she and Eli got into the car, she was still blinking sleep from her eyes as her husband pulled down the icy driveway and headed toward Lake Marion. It was going to be a long day, and she was starting to regret her promise to go ice fishing with Eli and Reggie. There was no backing out now, though. She was committed, and she was going to see this thing through if she froze to death trying to do it.

Even though it was early, the nursing home had already started its day. Early morning staff were hurrying about their jobs when Candice and Eli got there, and a handful of residents were gathered in the common area, watching the morning news. Reggie was one of them. He spotted them and waved almost as soon as they came in. Candice walked over to him while Eli went to the front office to sign him out.

"Are you excited?" he asked, grinning at her. He had a pile of equipment on the couch next to him.

"Well, I'm not really looking forward to the cold, but it will certainly be an experience," Candice said. "It will be nice to spend the day with you and Eli."

"It will be lovely," Reggie said. "I don't get to see the two of you nearly enough. I'm not blaming you or trying to guilt you into visiting me more," he added quickly. "You've got your own lives to lead, and it's lovely that you visit me as often as you do. But it will be nice to spend a day with family."

Candice smiled at him. The cold aside, he was right; it would be nice to spend an entire day together like this. Hadn't she just been thinking how nice it would be to do something other than what had become her daily routine? Sure, if she was coming up with activities this wouldn't be quite how she chose to spend the day, but in a way it didn't matter exactly what they did, as long as they were doing it together.

Eli returned from the front office with a bag of medication and a laminated schedule. He was grinning as much as Reggie was.

"I'm going to go put all your stuff in the car," he said. "Then I'll come back and Candice and I will help you out to the parking lot. It's a bit icy; I don't think they've salted it yet this morning."

"Go on then, hurry up. My freedom is so close I can taste it." He waved Eli away and, laughing, Eli grabbed the stuff off the couch and went outside. Candice sat down next to Reggie.

"Eli has been so excited about this trip," she told him. "He's really looking forward to it."

"I'm glad," Reggie said. "We've done this every year for most of his life. Ever since he was big enough to hold a fishing pole. Well, other than the year he was in the hospital."

"I think he would be more than happy to forget about that year," Candice said.

"I'm so glad he recovered as well as he did," Reggie said, looking fondly toward the door where his grandson had disappeared. "He's so young. He doesn't know how lucky he is."

"I think he might," Candice said softly. She hated thinking back to seeing Eli in the hospital, coughing from smoke inhalation and wearing casts and braces across the lower half of his body. It had not been a good time for either of them.

The door opened again, letting Eli in. He headed right over to them and offered Reggie his arm to help him up. Candice followed them toward the door, holding each set open for them, then when they were outside, she stepped up next to Reggie and took his other arm. Together, they guided him across the parking lot. The car was still running, and they settled Reggie into the front seat.

"Hold on," Eli said. "I've got something for you. It should help out on the ice."

He opened the trunk and returned with a pair of snow cleats, designed to fit over any shoe. He stretched them over the soles of Reggie's boots.

"More grip never hurts. I've got pairs for Candice and I as well."

"Good," Reggie said. "The last thing any of us needs today is a fall."

It was starting to get light out by the time they reached the lake. Candice waited in the car while Eli ventured out onto the ice, checking every few steps to make sure it was safe. He was wearing a head lamp, and she could see the bright beam marking his path across the lake.

He had scoped out the lake a few days ago, and had decided on the spot based on a recommendation from a friend, who had had luck catching fish there earlier that week. Luckily, it wasn't terribly far from where they had parked, and it didn't take very long for him to set up the shanty where they would be waiting. He came back to the car and grabbed the rest of the equipment from the trunk. This time, Candice helped him carry everything out to their little spot on the lake.

"Can you start setting the chairs up while I go get Reggie?" he asked. She nodded and got to work, rolling an insulated mat out on the floor of the shanty before setting up the folding chairs. There was just enough room for the three of them. The cooler, which was filled with warm soups and coffee, would have to wait outside.

By the time he and Reggie made it out to the shanty, Candice had their little space set up, complete with blankets hung over the back of the chairs for each of them. Her own chair had a book on it, and a pile of hand warmers. She was determined to stay nice and toasty during this outing.

Eli settled Reggie down in the middle chair and tucked the blanket over his lap. He had brought the bag of medications as well, and tucked them into the back corner of the shanty.

"Are you comfortable?" he asked his grandfather.

"You betcha," Reggie said. "I could sit here all day. Now, let's get the hole made and set the poles up. I need to catch something, so I have a good fishing story to tell once we get back to the nursing home."

Chuckling, Eli grabbed the auger from where he had placed it down outside the shanty and walked a few paces away from the chairs. Candice watched as he brushed away the snow on top of the ice and placed the drill bit down. He began spinning the auger, slowly forming a hole in the ice.

Candice helped him scoop out the shards of ice until they had a clean, round hole opening into the dark water. He made a second hole not far away, and then a third. All three of them dropped their lines in the water and settled back down on their chairs to wait. Thankfully, the shanty blocked most of the wind, and with all of her layers, Candice was plenty warm. Her book was waiting on her lap, but for the time being she was content to watch the line in the water.

As the sun rose, Eli and Reggie sank into a conversation about their past fishing trips. Candice tuned them out eventually and began fiddling with her line, bobbing it up and down and tugging on it a bit, wondering if the movement might make the fish more likely to bite. When she felt the hook catch on something, she nearly jumped out of her seat.

"I've got something," she said, standing up and beginning to pull the line in. Whatever it was, it felt big.

"Awesome job, Candice," Eli said. He walked over to help her reel it in. After a few minutes, she gave the pole over to him entirely. Her arms were getting tired.

"This is weird," Eli said as he tugged on the line. "The fish isn't fighting at all. You might have snagged a log or something. I think we've almost got it –"

He gave the line one last tug, and it jerked to a halt suddenly. Water splashed up out of the hole in the ice. Eli handed the pole back over to Candice and grabbed his net out of the shanty, then walked over to the hole.

"Okay, let it out a little. The fish or stick or whatever it is must be at the wrong angle to come through the hole. I'm just going to see if I can feel it with the net –"

With a gasp, he backpedaled from the hole he had been crouching over, dropping the net in the snow and falling on his rear.

"What happened?" Candice asked, still keeping hold of the pole.

"It's not a fish," he said, his eyes wide. "It's a dead body."

CHAPTER 5

CANDICE DROPPED her fishing pole in horror, and the body the hook had snagged must have started to sink, because the pole began sliding toward the hole in the ice. Eli reached out and grabbed it before it could fall into the water.

"Call the police," he said, looking pale and frightened.

She turned back toward the shanty and took her phone from Reggie, who had grabbed it from her chair and was holding it out to her. Still blinking in shock from the fact that she had somehow reeled in a dead body, she turned on the phone screen after stripping off her gloves, and stared in dismay at the blinking no service warning in the top right corner of her phone screen.

"I'm going to have to go closer to the shore," she said. "I'll be as quick as I can."

She was grateful for the snow cleats as she hurried across the lake. They bit into the ice and kept her from slipping and sliding as she hurried. She knew it was dangerous to walk across the frozen water without checking each step, but she would just have to trust that with how cold it had been recently, the lake would be thoroughly frozen. She watched her phone screen and when she saw the first bar of service, she stopped and called the emergency number.

She explained, stumbling over her own words, about the body and gave directions as best she could. They were parked in a small lot next to a more secluded beach on the shores of Lake Marion, and thankfully were the only shanty nearby, though she could see a few other people further out on the lake and further down the shore ice fishing as well.

The incident reported, all she had left to do was wait. She shuffled back and forth, trying to keep warm, wondering whether it would be better to go back to the shanty to wait, or stay where she was so she could wave the police over.

Thankfully, she didn't have long to wait – one of the benefits of living in such a small town. She saw a patrol car pull into the parking lot and park next to Eli's vehicle. She waved as she saw the pair of officers get out. They saw her and started heading across the lake toward her, moving slowly and carefully across the ice. One of them slipped and she winced, but he didn't go down.

Once they reached her, she led the way over to where Eli and Reggie were by the shanty. Eli was still holding onto the pole, staring at the hole with a horrified look on his face. Candice hesitated, not sure what she should do, but decided to go back over to Reggie, who looked plenty worried himself. She didn't really want to see the body, after all, and she would just be in the way as the police figured out what to do.

It turned out removing a body from under the ice was more difficult than she could have thought. The police managed to attach ropes to it to make sure it didn't sink back below the surface, since they didn't trust the fishing line not to break. Once they had secured the body, they radioed in for backup. Candice, Eli, and Reggie all waited by the shanty. They would be needed for questioning, she knew, but first the police would have to see just what they were dealing with.

One of the officers came over to them. "If you want to go wait in your car, go ahead," he said, looking at Reggie in concern. "This might take a while, and there's no reason you should freeze while you wait for us. We will need to take statements, so please don't leave. Please leave all of your items here for the time being. This is technically a crime scene, and we may need to comb through the area for evidence."

"Can I grab my grandfather's medications?" Eli asked, "He needs to take some in about an hour."

The officer looked through the bag quickly, then handed it over Eli. "I'll walk back to the vehicle with you," he said.

The four of them made their way back across the ice. Eli started the car and he, Candice, and Reggie sat inside, warming themselves in front of the vents while they watched as more police officers arrived.

The officers worked together to break the ice and Candice could see them drag the body up out of the lake, though they were far enough away that she couldn't see any details.

"I hate ice fishing," she said quietly.

"I've got the feeling that none of us will look at it quite the same way again," Eli said, just as quietly.

"When I said I wanted a story to tell at the nursing home, I didn't mean something like this," Reggie added.

She watched as the police took a record of the crime scene. While they took pictures, an ambulance pulled into the small parking lot, and two paramedics got out with a stretcher, which they hurried out across the ice. They covered the body with a sheet before carrying the stretcher back, but as they walked through parking lot, part of the sodden sheet slipped off the man, revealing his face. Candice jerked back, knocking her elbow against the center console.

"It's Rudolph," she hissed.

Eli and Reggie looked over to where the body was and Reggie made a low, sad sound. Eli frowned.

"The poor man," he said quietly. "I thought that he had just wandered off – or maybe had gone out with a relative and forgot to check out. I was so sure they were going to find him alive and well."

"He must've fallen into the lake," Candice said, feeling sad. "I feel so bad for him."

She remembered how vibrant and alive he had seemed when she'd met him. She wondered if he had some sort of disease that affected his decision making, like Alzheimer's. If he had missed a round of medication, and had gotten confused about something, that could explain why he had wandered out of the nursing home and onto the lake. She closed her eyes. She didn't want to think about it anymore.

They were still waiting in the car when more police arrived. Most of the officers were spread out on the lake, questioning the other fisherman and combing the ice for any evidence that might point toward what had happened to the old man. The original two officers came over to the car and knocked on the window.

"We'd like to get those statements now," the lead one said. "We'll ask you each some questions separately, and then we will let you get going. I'll have to talk to the detective to make sure, but I think it would be all right if we packed up your stuff for you so you can take it home. We have evidence that the body entered the lake elsewhere. We just need to know what happened today so we have it on record."

Eli went first, and they took turns talking to the officers outside of the vehicle. Reggie was last, but he took the least amount of time, and by the time they were all done, one of the officers had come back to the car with all of their equipment. The only thing the police were keeping was the fishing pole that had snagged the body, just in case there was some evidence somewhere on the hook or line.

They packed the vehicle up, and with a final okay from the police, Eli pulled out of the parking lot. He drove slowly back toward the nursing home. None of them said anything as the vehicle moved slowly through the town's snowy roads. After all, what could they possibly say in a situation like this?

CHAPTER 6

NEWS ABOUT RUDOLPH GRANGER'S death spread quickly, and unfortunately Candice and Eli's names were mentioned in the article. She didn't know how the reporter had gotten them, and silently wished that she could curse whoever had tipped them off with many stubbed toes and minor inconveniences in their future.

The story wasn't good for the nursing home, either. The scenario that the majority of the articles were running with was that Rudolph had simply wandered off, confused due to either his general senility or a missed dose of medication. Why he had gone to the lake was something no one knew, but everyone liked to guess on.

It was all speculation, of course, and was presented as such. The police hadn't issued any official report on the matter, and the nursing home itself was staying silent as well. She was sure that they had their own team of lawyers looking everything over. If they really were at fault, the consequences would be terrible for them. Candice hoped that they didn't get shut down. Even if one of the staff members had forgotten to give Rudolph his medication or if one of them had been too distracted to notice him walking right out the front door, it didn't mean that the entire place was bad. Reggie was happy there, as were a lot of the other residents, and it was also the only nursing home in the area. If it closed down, where would everyone go? Reggie could come and stay with her and Eli, of course, but many of the other residents didn't have opportunities like that.

Monday night, after a busy day at work during which most of the people who stopped in at the shop simply wanted to ask her about Rudolph, was a long since scheduled dinner with her parents. After such a long day, she was glad to pull up to her mother's house. She always enjoyed dinner with her parents, and tonight would be no exception, despite how tired she was. She'd never actually lived in the stone house, though she had stayed there temporarily on occasion, but it still felt like home to her. It was a small house, with only two bedrooms, two bathrooms, a living room, and a kitchen. The property, however, was large, with five wooded acres and a fenced in area behind the house for the dogs to run around.

Her mother owned two large dogs; a German Shepherd named Maverick and an Irish wolfhound named Keeva. Both had come to her mother by chance, and over the years, both had done their part to keep the family safe. Candice was always happy to see them, and that went doubly so today, after the stress of finding out she was featured in the latest news. She spent a few minutes petting them before making her way to the kitchen, where the rest of her family had gathered.

The table was already set, with a picturesque roast chicken sitting in the center, flanked by a plate of roasted halved redskin potatoes and a bowl of freshly made salad. Each of the plates had a half full glass of red wine next to it.

"This looks lovely, Mom," she said. "What's the occasion?" She had been expecting leftover soup from the deli, not something that looked like it could be served on Christmas.

"After hearing what happened on your fishing expedition, we figured you guys might want a little break from reality," David said. "I met a guy a couple months ago who makes his own wine, and this is a bottle I got from him. It's some of the best I've tasted. You'll have to let me know if you like it."

"I'm excited to try it," Candice said, taking a seat next to Eli. David cut the chicken, while Eli told them the story of what had happened at the lake.

"We haven't heard anything from the police since," he finished. "I guess it probably isn't realistic to expect an update on the case from them. I just wish we knew the truth behind what happened. Reggie says that he can't imagine Rudolph just wandering off like that. He, along with some of the other residents, are convinced something else is going on. There have been rumors of foul play floating around the nursing home."

"Is there any proof behind the rumors?" David asked as he placed some of the chicken on Candice's plate.

"Not as far as I know," Eli said with a sigh. "Apparently he had a falling out with his daughter, which seems to be where most of the rumors are coming from, but according to Reggie it was just a normal argument; nothing major or dramatic. Though Rudolph did have a history with one of the other residents there. She was obsessed with him, but he wanted nothing to do with her. A few people think she might've been behind it. She's just a generally nasty woman though, so people are eager to believe the worst about her. Someone also mentioned that he had an old business partner that things went south with years ago. Reggie told me he was going look more into that. I think he likes having a reason to dig around for answers."

"That's the first I've heard about that last one," Candice said. She took a sip of her wine. It was good; sweet and crisp, just like she preferred.

"I stopped in during lunch today," Eli told her. "I wanted to see how things were going. Apparently Reggie has been quite the center of attention since he got back from the fishing trip."

"Well, he did say he wanted a good fishing story to tell," Candice said.

"He may have gotten a bit more than he expected with this one," Eli said with a small smile. "He's been mobbed ever since he returned. I think he'd be enjoying it more if it wasn't for the circumstances."

"Hopefully the police release a statement soon to clear things up," Moira said. "I just wish that you weren't at the center of all this, Candice. I know it's not your fault, but this family can never get a break. You should be able to just focus on your life without having to deal with missing people and dead bodies."

"It was just bad luck," Candice said. "Anyway, it was a good thing. If we hadn't gone fishing at that exact spot, Rudolph might not have been found until spring, or ever. At least this way, his family can get some closure and he can be laid to rest. It's scary to think how easily people can just disappear."

The mood became somber after that, until Eli asked David how things were going at the brewery. Glad to think of something else for a while, Candice listened closely as she enjoyed the succulent chicken. David had been right; sometimes a break from reality was just the thing she needed.

CHAPTER 7

Speculation about Rudolph and what he had been doing on the lake ran rampant for the next few days. Allison had overheard a few nasty rumors that Candice had something to do with it. Candice knew it was mostly just due to the fact that she was there when the body had been found, but she also had a feeling that the rumors wouldn't exist if it wasn't for the candy shop's somewhat speckled past. She tried not to take it to heart, but it still hurt that the towns-folk could think that of her.

Nonetheless, Candice kept a smile pasted on her face whenever she was at work for the next few days. She tried to remain unfailingly polite, even when people asked her too-personal questions about the day Rudolph's body had been dredged up from the lake.

By the time Thursday rolled around, Candice was aching for the weekend. It had been almost a week since the incident, and the police still hadn't released any sort of official statement, other than to confirm that yes, a body had been found, and that the investigation was ongoing. They also noted that they currently had no suspects or people of interest in the case. She supposed that had been their way of trying to calm down some of the speculation, but it hadn't really worked. People had seemed to take the statement to mean that absolutely anyone could be a suspect, instead of no one being one. The majority of people still seemed convinced that the nursing home was at fault. Candice wasn't sure what to think; mostly she just wanted the rampant rumors to die down.

That Thursday, it was only her and Logan in the candy shop. He had been her first employee, and he knew the place as well as she did. He was also the only person Candice trusted completely in the kitchen. She was happy to give him some time to experiment with new recipes while she kept the front of the shop running, and was reasonably certain he wasn't going to set anything on fire or burn a pot full of sugar. Experimenting with new recipes was how they came up with new products to offer, and she was usually happy to let all of her employees have a go at it if they showed interest.

It was only a few hours before close when the door opened and in walked a somewhat familiar face. It took Candice a moment to place the woman. When she realized that she was Rudolph's daughter, Emmy, who she had spotted only briefly at the nursing home, all of her attention shifted toward her.

The woman, in contrast, seemed unable to focus on anything. Her gaze floated around the candy shop until she got closer to the register. There, she looked at Candice as if barely seeing her.

"I'd like to order a tasteful collection of chocolates for my father's wake," the woman said.

Candice blinked. "I'd be happy to help you, of course. May I ask why chocolates?"

"He always liked chocolate," Emmy said with a shrug. "It was his thing. He liked dark chocolate best, but a mix of dark and milk chocolate would be okay, since not everyone likes dark. The funeral is next

Wednesday. Do you think you could have maybe two-hundred of them ready by then?"

"Of course," Candice said. "We'll put a rush on the order. Do you have any particular flavors or designs you want?"

The other woman shook her head. "Just do a variety, so people can pick out what they like. Oh, and the order's for Emmy Baumer, if you need a name."

"I know," Candice said with a gentle smile, taking out a piece of paper to write the information down on. "I met you at the nursing home."

The women seemed to actually focus on her for the first time. She blinked. "Oh, you did. I remember you. You were sitting with my father before I got there, weren't you?"

"That was me," she agreed.

To her surprise, the other woman's eyes filled with tears. "I feel so terrible that the very last time I saw him, I was late for dinner, and we ended the night with an argument. I'm never going to forgive myself for that."

"I don't want overstep, since I obviously don't know

you or your father or anything about your relationship, but I know if he's anything like my mom and stepdad are, he would've forgiven you in a heartbeat."

The other woman sniffed. "You're probably right. I just wish I could go back in time and undo it all. I also wish I had rearranged my life to let him stay with me instead of sending him to that nursing home. As soon as the will is read, I'm going to use the money I inherit to hire a lawyer and sue them for everything I can."

"You think they were at fault then?" Candice hedged.

"Of course," the other woman said, her eyes darkening. "Their job was to keep him safe and they failed at it. It's their fault that I don't have a father anymore."

Candice wasn't sure how to reply to that, and she was saved from having to by the door opening again, this time letting in another familiar face in the form of Mr. Smith. The old man walked over to where his ginger candies were shelved and picked out a handful. He turned toward the counter, then froze. His eyes narrowed.

"You," he hissed, raising a hand to point at Emmy. "I know what you did. You're nothing but a greedy murderer. I don't know how you're brave enough to show your face in town, after killing your own father."

He looked like he was about to spit on her, and Candice quickly stepped between them.

"Mr. Smith!" she said sharply. "That's enough. I won't let you talk to my customers like that. You can wait over there in silence while I help—" She turned back to the woman, but broke off when she saw that Emmy was already backing away, her eyes wide with horror.

"I'll call about the order," she said quickly, then turned and fled out the door.

CHAPTER 8

SHE WAS UNSETTLED from the encounter with Mr. Smith when she got home that evening. On the one hand, it was difficult to take him seriously when she knew how he was with her. He had been accusing her of things for so long that she had the temptation to dismiss anything he said.

However, she had seen firsthand just how upset he was about his missing friend. She knew that they must have been relatively close. Was it possible that he knew something about the man's relationship with his daughter that no one else did? Accusing someone of murder was a pretty big leap to make if one didn't have any good reason to believe they were right.

When she told Eli about it, he dismissed it with a wave. "You know how he is," he said. "How can you take anything he says seriously? I don't even know why you still let him come around. He's a toxic person, Candice. You shouldn't let him do to someone else what he's been doing to you."

Candice didn't quite agree with Eli. She had seen see a different side to Mr. Smith recently, and wondered how much more to him there was. But she didn't pursue it. It was late and she was tired, and all she wanted to do was sit back and relax and put something halfway nutritious in her complaining stomach. Luckily for her, Eli had once again made dinner; this time it was oven baked trout, mashed cauliflower, and asparagus.

"Maybe you should open your own restaurant, instead of a doggy bakery," she said as she savored the perfectly cooked fish.

"Nah, I've seen cooking shows. I know just how stressful that would be," Eli said. "I like cooking, but just as a hobby."

"Well, I'm very glad it's a hobby you decided to pick up. Thank you. It means a lot to me that you will almost always have dinner ready when I get home." They ate in silence for a few moments before she asked, "How is the loan for the bakery coming, anyway?"

"I'm still waiting for the bank to get back to me," he said. "The agent I spoke to seemed positive about it, though. Once I get the loan, I can start seriously looking into locations for the bakery itself and reaching out to potential places to sell the treats. I've been compiling some recipes. Pretty soon I'm going to put together my first batch and see how Keeva and Maverick like them."

"I'm sure they'll be happy to be your test subjects," she said with a smile.

"Me too," he said, chuckling. "By this time next year, we should be open and running. I'm really excited."

"Me too," she said. "This is going to be great for you."

"For both of us," he said.

Candice smiled just thinking about it. Both of them self-employed, working at jobs that they were passionate about. She couldn't think of anything better. Still, there were niggling concerns in the back of her mind. Once things settled down again, would she still feel that terrible dread about having a routine? What about when Eli started working just as long of hours as she did? Would their relationship suffer when they had to argue over who made dinner and who tidied the house? How much would things change with both of them working full time jobs? It wasn't easy keeping a business running, even if it was something they were passionate about. She had lots of days when she would get home dead tired, with barely enough energy to eat dinner and stay awake while they watched some television before bed. Would things change for the worse when both of them had days like that?

On the other hand, they had made it through worse, and she knew that even if it might take a bit of practice, they would get through whatever changes were coming in the future as well.

After dinner, they spent a pleasant evening in front of the TV before heading up to bed. It had been an emotionally draining few days, and they were both exhausted. Tomorrow it would have been a week exactly since they found the body. Part of her wished she could go back in time and demand they fished in another spot, but then she reminded herself that it was better for everyone involved that Rudolph was found. She didn't want to think about the anguish his daughter would feel over the coming years if he had never been found.

She fell asleep quickly, but was woken just a few hours later by the incessant ringing of a phone. She groped blindly at her bedside table for her cell phone, but the screen was dark when she picked it up. Her phone wasn't the one ringing.

"Eli," she muttered, elbowing her husband. "Eli, someone's calling you."

He woke with a sleepy mutter and grabbed the phone off his table. She heard his tired "Hello?" She could also hear faint voice on the other end of the phone as someone replied, but it was too quiet for her to tell who it was. She got her answer soon enough. "Reggie?" He sat up in bed. "Slow down. Are you all right? Of course. We'll be right over."

He put the phone down and turned to look at Candice. She could just see his outline in the dark. "That was Reggie," he said unnecessarily. "He said he thinks someone is trying to kill him."

CHAPTER 9

CANDICE QUICKLY PULLED on a sweater and a coat over her pajamas and stuffed her feet into boots. She and Eli didn't spare time to talk as they rushed out to the car. He started the engine and jerked the gearshift into drive all in one motion, then drove down the dark driveway as quickly as he dared.

"Did he say exactly was going on?" she asked.

"He mentioned something about someone messing with his medicine," he told her. "He sounded confused. I don't know exactly what's going on, but something is definitely wrong. I would just call the nursing home, but I'm not sure how much I trust them anymore."

"At least it isn't too far," Candice said. "I hope everything's okay when we get there."

It was the middle of the night, which meant that instead of just using the keypad to enter the code and let themselves in, they had to press the buzzer for the front office. A sleepy looking staff member came to the door to let them in. "We don't usually allow visitors this late," she told them, looking at them unhappily.

"I got an urgent call from my grandfather," Eli explained. "I want to see him."

Looking irritated but too tired to really care, she waved to them down the hall. "Just remember to buzz me when you're ready to leave, or else the alarm will sound," she told them.

Eli called out an affirmative as he hurried down the hall. Candice followed him just a little bit more slowly. They both knew the way to Reggie's room by heart. The door was shut when they got there, but it opened as soon as Eli knocked. Reggie must have been waiting by it. He looked more frightened than Candice could remember seeing him.

"Come on in," he said, hurrying them inside and then shutting the door behind them.

"What happened?" Eli asked, looking around the room as if expecting to see an attacker there.

"Someone switched all of my pills with sugar pills," Reggie said. "I saved them all. They're on my nightstand."

Candice and Eli followed Reggie into the bedroom. A small plastic cup of pills was on the nightstand. Eli dumped them out across the surface of the small table and looked at them closely. Frowning, he lifted to his mouth and touched the tip of his tongue to it.

"You're right; they're just sugar pills," he said, frowning. "How long has this been going on, Reggie?"

"I'm pretty sure this is the first night it has happened," Reggie said. "I tasted the difference right away. I always put the pills in my mouth and let them sit there for a second or two while I grab my cup of water. As soon as I realized the problem with this batch, I called you."

"You did the right thing," Eli said.

"This means that someone here is trying to hurt

you," Candice said, shaken. "The medications are pretty strictly regulated, aren't they?"

"They are," Eli said grimly. "I'm not sure what to think about this."

"That's why I called you instead of contacting someone from the office," Reggie said. "What should we do now? I need my medication. It's not safe to quit some of it cold turkey."

"First things first, we're getting you out of here," Eli said. "Pack a bag with what you absolutely need tonight, and tomorrow we can come back to get whatever else you might need. I'm going to go to the office and see if I can get your pills – your actual pills this time. I'll need you to look through them and make sure they're the right ones."

Reggie nodded, still looking scared. "I'll help you pack," Candice said. Eli gave her a quick smile of gratitude and hurried out the door, sweeping the sugar pills into his hand.

Candice followed Reggie's instructions to find a small carry-on in the closet. She helped him pack his clothes for the morning, and gathered up his toiletries. It didn't take very long, and the two of them returned to the main living area to wait. She knew Eli wanted to get out of there as quickly as possible. She didn't blame him. This was scary. Someone had either purposely switched Reggie's medication, or the staff was so negligent that they didn't notice the difference.

"Sorry for waking you two up," Reggie said as they waited.

"There's nothing to be sorry for," she said. "I'm glad you called us. We're going to get to the bottom of this, I promise."

"Do you think this is related to what happened to Rudolph?" he asked.

She hesitated. "I don't know. It would be such a coincidence if it didn't, but why would someone be targeting you because of that?"

"I don't know," Reggie said. "I don't see how I could be a threat to anyone. I barely knew the man; he hadn't lived here for that long when he disappeared."

"Maybe they think you know more than you do," Candice said, sighing. Before she could say anything more, the door to the room opened and Eli walked in. He had a bag like the one they had been given for Reggie's medications during the fishing trip, but looked grim.

"I managed to speak to the pharmacist on staff," he said. "I may have made a mistake by letting him have most of the pills, but he said he wanted to match them to the ones they keep in stock. I pocketed one just in case the police need it for some reason; I plan on going to them in the morning. I hate not knowing if I can trust the people who work here. I thought this was a good place, but now I'm not so sure."

"It is," Reggie said, frowning. "Or, it has been. I can't complain about how things have been for the past few years. I'm sure it's just one bad apple."

"Well, until they find that bad apple, I don't want you staying here," Eli said. "Let's go home. We'll get you set up in the guest room. Tomorrow, we'll come back and see what else we can do."

They made their way through the nursing home to the front door, and Eli pressed the buzzer until a staff member came to let them out. She must have been told what was going on, because she didn't say anything to them as they left.

Once again, Candice took the backseat as Reggie settled into the front. They were all tired enough that there wasn't much in the way of conversation on the way home, and they made a beeline for the guest room when they got there. Candice placed the carry-on on top of the chair in the corner while Eli pulled back the blankets and made sure the bed wasn't too dusty.

"Do you need anything else?" Eli asked his grandfather. "What about a glass of water?"

"Honestly, I just want to get some sleep," Reggie said. "I'm exhausted."

"I am too," Eli admitted. "Well, we'll be just down the hall. If you need anything, holler. We can figure out what to do next in the morning."

Candice said her own goodnight to Reggie, then trailed after Eli back to the bedroom. Even though she was exhausted, she had a feeling she was going to be sleeping lightly tonight. There was too much to think about for her to be able to get any real rest.

CHAPTER 10

C\textsc{andice woke} with a start early the next morning. It almost felt like the night before had been a dream, but the sound of two voices floating up the stairs convinced her it had been real. Someone had tried to sabotage Reggie's medication. She couldn't say for certain that they had meant to kill him — she was pretty sure someone would have noticed before any real damage was done, and as far as she knew, missing one or two doses might make him confused and muddled, but it probably wouldn't be fatal. She just wished she knew why.

She forced herself to get out of bed even though she was still tired. She wouldn't get any answers by laying around. By the sound of it – and the smell of it – Eli and Reggie were busy making breakfast down in the kitchen. She felt a bit bad for sleeping as late as she had, but told herself that if they needed her Eli would have woken her up.

Felix, ever her loyal friend, followed her as she padded down the stairs, tying a bathrobe tightly around herself to help keep out the chill of the morning. Sure enough, the guys were in the kitchen making what looked like enough food for five people

"Did we invite an army over?" she asked with a yawn as she stood in the doorway. They both turned to look at her, breaking into very similar looking grins.

"We couldn't decide what to make, so we decided to make a little bit of everything," Eli told her.

"I'm looking forward to a break from the nursing home food," Reggie admitted. "This is real food."

"I thought everything at the nursing home was freshly made?" Candice asked as she walked over to the cupboard to take out a mug, then poured herself a cup of coffee.

"It's freshly made, but minus all the good stuff like

butter and salt and oil," Reggie said, wrinkling his nose. "It's not real food if it tastes too healthy."

"I told you, we're going easy on the salt and fats here too, Reggie," Eli said. "I trust the doctors there to know what your health needs are. We can cheat a little bit, but not too much. Wouldn't it be just great if I took you from the nursing home to keep you safe and then ended up rushing you to the hospital because you had a heart attack from too much bacon?"

"Ah, that's what the medication is for," Reggie said, waving a hand dismissively. "Besides, what's the point of being alive if you can't live a little sometimes?"

They continued arguing in a friendly sort of way as they finished making breakfast. Candice pitched in when it came time to flip the pancakes. They really had made a little bit of everything, and she knew there was no way they would finish it.

She made a note to pack up whatever they didn't eat and take it over to the brewery, where she could stash it in the mini fridge and surprise David when he got there later that day. He worked most weekends, and she was sure he would appreciate some homemade food instead of the usual packaged soups he kept there.

After breakfast, Candice cleaned up while Eli and Reggie went upstairs to get ready for the day. Once she was done cleaning the kitchen, she went back upstairs to wash her face and hair, and change her clothes.. She knew they had a busy day ahead of them. First things first, though; they had to return to the nursing home to pick up a few more things for Reggie if he was going to be staying any longer.

It was late morning by the time they all made it out to the car and Eli pulled out of the driveway. As they drew closer to the nursing home, Eli's good mood faded and he began to look more and more grim. By the time they pulled into the parking lot, he was glaring at the building as if it had personally done him some grievous wrong.

"Let's go talk to the director," Candice said, putting her hand on his shoulder. "She might have some answers."

All three of them trooped into the building. A few of the residents looked over and waved at Reggie, who waved back, looking pretty happy about the fact that he hadn't spent the night there. They went to the front office and were nearly ran over by the director as she was leaving it.

"Oh, just the people I wanted to see," she said, looking between the three of them. "I can be with you in five minutes if you'd like to go wait inside."

"Thanks, Ms. Leopold," Candice said. "We'd be happy to wait."

They settled into the office, Candice looking around with curiosity. The director was relatively new; she only been there for the last year. As far as Candice had noticed, she hadn't made any major changes, which she figured was a good thing, since the nursing home had already been doing pretty well. She hadn't really spoken to her beyond a few words of greeting here and there, and wondered how she would handle something major like this.

She didn't have long to wait. The director came back before the promised five minutes were up, and shut the door firmly behind her.

"We're taking this very seriously," she said as she settled into her seat behind her desk. "We're launching a full internal investigation. Only a limited number of people have access to the medication, and we are going to be examining each of them very thoroughly. Have you contacted the police?"

"Not yet," Eli said.

"I'd ask that you wait on that until we finish with our own investigation," she said. "Of course, it's up to you. I understand if you feel the need to contact them. What happened was very serious."

"I can't promise that I'll wait, but I'll think about it," he said. "What should we do in the meantime?"

"Well, I can tell you that we are taking certain precautions, including a two-person verification system for any medication that is handed out. Two people have to sign off that it's the right medication, and then they both have to watch as the resident takes it. I can guarantee you that what happened with Reggie won't happen again, but I understand if you're uncomfortable with him being here for now. If he would prefer to stay with you for a few days, that's perfectly fine." She smiled at Reggie. "It probably has the added benefit of being a fun vacation, too."

"Well you'll have no complaints from me if I get to stay with my grandson and his wife," Reggie said. "I just don't want to put you two out." He looked between them.

"You're not," Candice said quickly. "I'm more than happy to have you stay with us for as long as you need."

"Well, it sounds like that's settled," Mrs. Leopold said. "I'll go speak to our medical personnel and arrange for them to give you the next few days' worth of his medication along with the schedule. I'll also talk to a nurse and get you a dietary sheet drawn up. I'll find you in about twenty minutes with the information and medication."

Before she left the room, the director shook each of their hands and apologized once again for what she called the medication mix-up. She left the three of them alone just outside her office.

"I'm not sure what to think about –" Eli started, but he broke off when a grey haired woman came up to Reggie and wrapped him in a hug, sobbing. Surprised, Reggie pulled back.

"Lainey," he said. "What are you doing?"

"I heard what happened," she said. "And then when you weren't in your room this morning I thought you were dead. Just like Rudolph. I was beside myself."

Somewhat awkwardly, Reggie patted her on the shoulder. Candice tried to hide her smirk. She knew that Reggie didn't particularly like the woman, but he was polite enough not to push her away.

"I'm going to be gone for a couple of days," he said. "I promise, though, I'm still alive and kicking." He chuckled. "You're not going to get rid of me that easily."

CHAPTER 11

IT ENDED up being a pleasant weekend. The three of them spent a lot of family time together, laughing and cooking, and on Sunday evening in lieu of their usual meal at the nursing home, they all went to dinner at the Red Cedar Grill. Candice was almost sad to go into work on Monday morning, but she had that big order of chocolates to finish for Emmy, and she had a new idea for a limited seasonal chocolate design that she wanted to experiment with when she was done.

Allison was working with her that day, and her half-sister was more than happy to take over the register while Candice buried herself in the kitchen. She only had twenty more of the chocolates to make.

This last batch was dark chocolate with sea salt sprinkled on top and a rich raspberry filling. She had done her best to make a good variety, with twenty plain dark chocolates, twenty plain milk chocolates, twenty of each with a nougat filling, twenty of each with a caramel filling, twenty of each with nuts, and last but not least, twenty of each with the raspberry filling. She hoped Emmy would be happy with it. She hadn't given her many details of what she wanted besides mentioning a variety.

She poured her soul into the chocolates as she made them, wanting everything to be perfect. She couldn't imagine what Rudolph's daughter was going through right now, and she definitely didn't want to be the one to make the day of the funeral harder for her.

It didn't take her that long to finish the last batch. Once the chocolates were cooling, she turned her attention to the new idea she'd had over the weekend. She wished she had thought of it earlier in the season; white chocolate snowmen were the perfect winter offering, after all.

White chocolate was something Candice had grown to like over the past few years. She still preferred a nice, creamy milk chocolate, but she'd worked with white chocolate enough that she could whip up a recipe from memory alone.

Once the bowl of warm, melted chocolate was ready, she took the silicon half-sphere molds out and carefully painted the insides with the chocolate before putting them in the fridge. While the half spheres were chilling, she made some white chocolate mousse and added coconut shavings to give it some texture and a hint of flavor besides white chocolate.

Once the molds had been chilled for long enough she remove them from the fridge and carefully peeled the silicon away from the chocolate. She'd made three different sizes, so this took her a while. She took her time filling half of the molds with the coconut white chocolate mousse. Then, with precision that made her hold her breath, she carefully touched the empty half-spheres to a hot pan just enough to melt very edge of the chocolate and then joined them together with the halves that were filled with mousse, creating perfectly round spheres with only a hint of a seam. By some miracle, she didn't break any of the fragile shapes.

Once this was done, she used the last of the warm

chocolate as glue to stack the spheres on top of one another, creating small snowmen three spheres high. Once she had a small army of them, she mixed some food coloring into melted sugar and painted on buttons, eyes, a smiling mouth, and an orange carrot nose. She wasn't sure how to make arms, and decided to ask Allison her opinion on that.

The end result was a snowman made out of three white chocolate truffles, standing a few inches tall. The completed one smiled cheerfully at her, and she grinned back at her newest creation. These would go right in the center of the largest glass display case, she decided. She could spruce them up a little too, with edible sugary glitter.

Feeling tired from the protracted focus she'd had to keep to create the snowmen, she decided to take a short break and go work the register with Allison. The fresh air would do her some good.

She was surprised to find a man she recognized there, chatting with Allison. He didn't seem to recognize her when she walked in, only glancing at her for a second as she entered the storefront. She had only seem him once before, at the nursing home, but his imposing figure was hard to forget.

"I need a gift basket for someone," he told them. "Something with a few different kinds of chocolate. I don't know what she likes. Do you offer anything like that?"

"We don't have any gift baskets premade," Allison said, "but we can put something together for you. Why don't you go around the store and pick out some chocolates that look good, and I'll go grab a gift basket from the back?"

She smiled at Candice as she left the register and headed for the back of the store. Candice took her place at the register. She wondered who the man was buying the gift basket for. From what Reggie had told her, he wasn't from town. For that matter, she wondered why he was still there at all. Then she realized that Rudolph's funeral was in just a few days; he was probably staying for that.

Allison returned just a couple minutes later with a gift basket and arranged it artfully with the chocolates. He seemed happy with his purchase, though Candice was kicking herself for not getting those white chocolate snowmen out sooner. He probably would have bought one of those as the centerpiece if she had. He seemed to have favored the more wintery pieces.

The door opened just as he was walking out and in came Eli and Reggie, two familiar faces that Candice was very happy to see.

"This is a nice surprise," she said. "Are you here to see me or for the candy?"

"Both," Eli said, grinning at her. "It's been a while since Reggie's seen the candy shop, so I thought he might want to look around. Do you have any of that peppermint fudge left?"

"Unfortunately, we don't," Candice said. "I do have something new I can show you though. I'll be right back."

She hurried into the kitchen to retrieve a white chocolate snowman and showed it to Eli and Reggie, who both seemed impressed by it. Allison looked over her shoulder as well, and shot Candice a thumb's up before grabbing a rag and some cleaning solution and heading toward the front windows.

"I'd feel bad eating this," Eli said. "It's like a work of art. All you need is a top hat for it."

"I thought of that, but I'm not quite sure how to make one out of something edible," Candice admitted. "I'll see if I can come up with something creative. I could order some silicon molds, I guess, but that would take weeks to get here and these will probably just be a seasonal thing, so I don't know if it's worth it."

"They're certainly cute," Eli said. "Is this the big project you mentioned earlier this morning?"

"No, those were the chocolates for Rudolph's funeral," Candice said.

"Oh, that reminds me," Reggie said, starting. "Can one of you take me? I was going to go along with a group from the nursing home, but since I won't be there..."

"Of course," Candice said. "I'll have to go there anyway to drop the chocolates off. It's no trouble at all, Reggie. We're happy to help."

CHAPTER 12

WEDNESDAY MORNING, she carefully boxed up all of the chocolates and put them in her car. Eli and Reggie were driving to the funeral separately, since she had to stop at the candy shop first and had volunteered to go to the funeral home a little bit early to help arrange the chocolates.

Candice's Candies didn't usually do catering, so she was a bit unprepared, but luckily she had been able to borrow some lovely decorative tiered trays from her mother. She was determined to do her part to make the day as easy as possible for Emmy.

The funeral service and wake were being held at the only small funeral home in town. Candice had never been there before, but she had driven past plenty of times. It was still a good hour before the wake was supposed to start, and there were only two other vehicles in the parking lot when she got there.

Emmy must have been waiting for her, because she met her at the door and held it open for her as Candice carried in the boxes of chocolates. She followed Candice out to the car to help bring in the trays, all in almost complete silence.

Inside the funeral home, lovely bouquets had already been arranged on the tables, along with pitchers of water. Whoever had set all of that up had left space for the chocolates. Candice set up the tiered display trays and carefully arranged the chocolates on them, setting up the little cards she had made that let people know what each variety of chocolate was. The last thing they needed was for someone to have an allergic reaction to one of the ingredients.

"Thank you so much," Emmy said. "This is gorgeous."

"It was my pleasure," Candice said.

She made herself scarce until people began to arrive, and found Eli and Reggie the parking lot to walk in with them. Beautiful, somber music was playing over loudspeakers and while she was gone, chairs had been set up facing the closed casket. Candice stuck close to Reggie and Eli, feeling a bit uncomfortable. She had never liked funerals very much, though she supposed that not many people did.

She spotted a group of people from the nursing home – all people who had gotten to know Rudolph during his short time there. Lainey was among them. Reggie started to go over to them, but when he saw her, he stopped in his tracks and moved to the other side of the room. Candice and Eli followed him, sharing an amused look.

"I don't want to risk her getting attached to me like she did to Rudolph," he muttered. "Apparently the fact that someone tried to poison me by switching out my medications makes me some sort of tragic hero. I can't believe she actually came up to me and hugged me the other day. We never got along that well in the past."

"You know, you're going to have to deal with her eventually," Eli said, looking amused.

They sat near the back, letting the people who had

known Rudolph better sit near the front. She saw another familiar face come through the doors just as the service was about to begin. It was Morgan, who looked much more somber than he had the other day at the candy shop.

"I wonder why he came," Reggie muttered, looking at the man. "I saw him at the nursing home a few times. They kept arguing about socks for some reason, it's the oddest thing. Rudolph told me he and his father are old family friends, but I think they had a falling out a while ago."

"Even if they weren't getting along, it makes sense that he'd come the funeral of someone he'd known for years," Candice said. "He stopped in the candy shop the other day, did I tell you that? He bought a gift basket for someone."

Reggie frowned, watching as Morgan took a seat up front, next to Emmy, and the service began. Candice tried to focus on listening to the story of Rudolph's life, instead of all of the questions she had about his death.

CHAPTER 13

AFTER THE FUNERAL, Emmy came over to Candice, Eli, and Reggie, and surprised Candice by pulling her into a quick hug.

"Thank you so much again for the chocolates," she said. "I didn't realize before – you're one of the people who found him, aren't you? I can't believe I didn't make the connection before. A friend mentioned it to me when I pointed you out to him after the service."

"I am," Candice admitted. "I'm sorry I didn't tell you."

"Oh, no, I'm sorry that I didn't realize. I would've never asked you to make the chocolates if I had. I'm sure finding him was hard for you, and it wasn't right for me to ask you to do something that might make you dwell on that. Thank you so much for finding him, though. I know you didn't mean to, but it means the world to me. If you hadn't... I might have spent the rest my life just wondering what had happened to him."

"I'm glad that we were able to give you closure," Candice said.

"It was nice to see you again, Reggie," she said, turning toward the older man. Behind her, Candice saw Morgan approach. He looked like he was about to interrupt, but seemed to decide against it when Emmy continued talking. "Rudolph spoke highly of you, even though I know he didn't know you for long."

"He seemed like a good man," Reggie said. "I wish I'd been able to get to know him better."

"Are you still staying at the nursing home? I was there the other day, picking up my father's things, and someone mentioned you had left."

"I'm staying with my family, but only for a while," he said. "It's a mini-vacation for me."

She nodded. "That's lovely, I'm sure the three of you are having a wonderful time. Well, you enjoy your day. Thank you once again, Candice. You've earned a lifelong customer. Thanks for everything you've done for me."

Before leaving, Eli asked Reggie if he wanted to stop by and say hi to the group from the nursing home, but his grandfather declined. "I see them quite enough as it is," he said. "Let's go home."

That sounded good to all of them. Candice had taken the day off for the funeral, leaving Suri and Logan to take care of the store. It felt weird, not being there on a weekday, but she trusted them. She had left Suri with instructions to make more of the snowmen and knew that her employee would likely do an even better job than she had. Suri was quite the artist, even if she didn't have the instinctive skill with cooking that Allison and Candice had. Logan was somewhere in between; he could follow directions well enough to make most recipes, but his real skill was with the customers. Candice thought they were a well-rounded team, and didn't know what she'd do if one of them left.

"Why didn't you tell Emmy about the medication?"

Eli asked as they pulled away from the funeral home. Candice blinked. She hadn't even caught that.

"I'm not sure I trust her," Reggie admitted. "Now, mind you, I'm not saying I think she's guilty of anything, but Rudolph had a lot of money and I know his daughter stood to inherit it all. She was the one who sent him to the nursing home, and she was the last one who saw him before he vanished. If she is behind it, I don't want her to know that they're investigating the medication thing."

"I didn't know that about the money," Eli said, frowning. "That would certainly be motive for murder, if that's what happened to him. I was going to hold off contacting the police like Mrs. Leopold asked me to, but now I don't know if I should."

"She's probably perfectly innocent," Reggie said. "And if she is, the last thing she needs is the police investigating her for her father's death. I'm just playing it safe, Eli. Pay no mind to a paranoid old man like me."

"I don't think you're paranoid," Eli said. "But I'll respect your wishes... for now. If the internal investigation of the nursing home doesn't turn up anything, we're going to have to go to the police with everything."

They spent the rest of the day lounging around at home. They played a couple of board games, then walked over to the brewery to say hi to David. It was a nice day, despite the fact that they had spent the morning at a funeral, and Candice was glad she had taken the entire day off. Family was something she'd never taken the time to appreciate much when she was younger, and as an adult, she was determined not to ever take it for granted.

She went to bed that night with her thoughts full of ideas for the candy shop. When she woke up, it was still dark out, and it took a while for her to identify what the painful needling sensation in her shoulder was. At last, feeling grouchy, she sat up and pushed Felix off of her.

"What are you doing, cat?" she asked. The cat made a sound halfway between a growl and a meow that she had never heard before and dug his claws back into her shoulder. She reached up to push him off again, then froze. She smelled smoke.

"Eli," she said, nudging him. "Eli, wake up." He

groaned and opened his eyes, and seemed to realize that something was wrong quicker than she had.

"Something burning?" he mumbled.

"It smells like it, and Felix is freaking out."

She had no sooner spoken than the smoke alarm in the hallway went off, and she heard Reggie shout from the other room. They both jumped up, hurrying into the hall. Eli shut off the smoke alarm while Candice went to check on Reggie.

"Is something on fire?"

"That's what we're trying to figure out," Candice said.

She hurried downstairs and saw, to her horror, the flickering light of flames through the living room window. The porch was on fire.

"We have to get out of here," she shouted. She heard Eli's footsteps upstairs as he went to get Reggie, and Candice crouched down to scoop the terrified cat into her arms.

They left the house out the back door as a group, and circled around to the front. Candice stared in horror at the raging flames on the porch. Her first thought was to grab the hose from the side of the house, but it had been taken in for winter and the pipes were probably frozen solid. She was frozen, staring at the flames, until Eli put his hand on her shoulder and gently pulled her toward the car. He had a phone pressed to his ear and seemed to be talking to an emergency dispatcher.

"The fire department will be here soon," he told her. "They want us to keep back from the house. Let's go wait in the car. Come on, there's nothing we can do." With one last look back at the house, she turned away from it and followed Eli toward the driveway.

CHAPTER 14

CANDICE HAD NEVER FELT SO helpless as she did then, watching the porch burn and being able to do nothing. It seemed to take forever for the firetruck to arrive, and then even longer for the flames to finally go out. When all that was left were the scorched, sodden remains of the porch and the blackened side of the house, one of the firemen came over to them with a grim look on his face.

"We're going to need to do a full arson investigation," he said. "We also need to check for structural and electrical damage before anyone is allowed back inside. Do you have somewhere you can stay for a couple of days?"

"You can come back to the nursing home with me," Reggie offered. "The couch has a pull-out bed."

"Thanks," Candice said, giving him a grateful look. "We'll stay there tonight, then we can probably stay with my mom and stepdad after that. Can we go back in to get our stuff?"

"Give one of my men a list of what you need and we'll get some of the basics for you as soon as we're sure the fire's not going to restart."

Eli and Candice nodded gratefully and the three of them gathered around the pad of paper the fireman handed them, writing down what they needed from inside. An hour later, they had a couple of duffel bags full of clothes, a carrier for Felix, and their cell phones, and had been sent on their way.

"At least the damage doesn't seem too bad," Eli said as he drove down the driveway.

"The porch is pretty much gone," she said.

"Yeah, but the house itself is fine, and we can rebuild the porch. What's important is that we're all okay."

"Yes, partially thanks to Felix. I can't believe he woke

me up when he smelled smoke. He's such a smart cat."

She peered through the holes in the carrier to check on him. He looked terrified, and she felt bad for him. He had no way to understand what was going on. She hardly understood what was going on herself. It had all happened so quickly.

"How are you doing?" Eli asked Reggie. His grandfather started, as if he had been lost deep in thought.

"Fine, I'm fine," he mumbled.

"No, you're not," Eli said. "You've been quiet this whole time. What are you thinking?"

"The fire is my fault," he said quietly.

"How on earth did you come to that conclusion?" Eli asked. "Somehow I doubt you went out there and started it yourself."

Reggie harrumphed. "Of course not, don't be ridiculous. But someone is obviously trying to kill me. First the medications, and now this. I'm a danger to you."

"No. Even if you're right and someone is after you,

they're the danger, not you. We're hardly going to abandon you just because someone might want to hurt you. I'm going to the police first thing in the morning. I've had enough of this internal investigation thing the nursing home is doing. It's time that the professionals got involved."

This was the second time in less than a week that they pulled into the nursing home parking lot late at night. It was a different staff member who buzzed them in this time, but she looked no less annoyed – that is, until she smelled the scent of smoke and saw their bedraggled appearances.

"We had a house fire," Eli said. "Reggie invited us to stay at his place for the night. I hope that's okay."

"Of course, of course," she said, her eyes wide. "Residents are always welcome to have guests. You three get settled. I'll see if I can go dig up a spare box for your kitty."

Grateful for her help, Candice followed Eli and Reggie back to Reggie's room, where he unlocked the door and stepped back to let them inside.

"Home sweet home," he said, and Candice thought that he seemed to mean it. No matter how much he liked spending time with them, this place really was his home and had been for the past few years.

"I'll get the couch set up," Eli said. "Do you either of you want to take a quick shower? We all smell like smoke."

"I should probably wait until she gets back with a box for Felix," she said, placing the carrier on the counter to give the cat a view of the room. He seemed a bit more relaxed now, thankfully.

They had the pullout couch ready by the time the staff member returned. She was carrying a cheap litter box and a bag of cat litter.

"Here you go. We keep a stash in case one of the residents runs out. You go ahead and set this up. I'll go grab some extra blankets for you, and some spare sweatpants and T-shirts. You look like you need them," she added, casting a look at their soot-stained clothed and the scantily clad pullout bed.

"That would be wonderful," Candice said. "Thank you so much."

She set up the litter box up and let Felix out, showing him where it was. She found a bowl to use for his water, and had made him a nice little area near the bathroom by the time she heard voices in the hall. She cracked the door open, thinking the woman who was helping them had returned, then paused when she realized it was two people in the middle of a conversation.

"Everything points toward her," one of the voices said. "She had access to the medication, she had a reason to want him gone, and I don't know if he would sneak out of here in the middle of the night for anyone but his daughter."

"It's so sad," the other voice said. "If you're right, that would have been such a horrible way to go. Killed by one of the people he loved the most."

"Mrs. Leopold is giving the report to the police in the morning. If they manage to corroborate everything, Emmy will hopefully be in jail by this time next week and the nursing home's name will be cleared. Let me tell you, as horrible as all this is, I'll be glad when we stop getting irate calls from our residents' relatives."

"Me too. Now, I better hurry and drop off these linens. The poor dears look so bedraggled. I have to

WHITE CHOCOLATE AND WORRIES

go do my rounds after that, but do you want to meet in the break room in half an hour?"

"You betcha. I'll save you one of those cookies you like so much."

Candice hurriedly shut the door again so she wouldn't be caught eavesdropping, only to open it again when someone knocked on it a few seconds later. She opened it to see the staff member bringing them the promised blankets and clothes.

"Thanks you so much," she said, hoping that nothing in her face gave away the fact that she had been spying on the woman.

"No problem at all," the other woman said, giving her a warm smile. "If you need anything else at all, don't hesitate to page the front office. Reggie can show you how. Have a good night."

With that, the door shut, and the three of them were left alone to get cleaned up and try to put the horrible night behind them.

CHAPTER 15

ONCE THEY HAD ALL SHOWERED, changed, and Felix was eating out of a tin of tuna on the floor, Candice told them what she had overheard.

"So, it sounds like they're going to go to the police tomorrow morning. Hopefully all of this will be over then."

"I don't know," Eli said. "I wonder what they found that makes them think the daughter did it. She seemed so nice."

"She did," Candice agreed with a frown. "They said she had access to the medication. I wonder how?"

"Speaking of that, did either of you bring my

medication?" Reggie asked distractedly. He was digging through one of the duffel bags.

Eli frowned and shook his head, looking at Candice questioningly.

"I didn't either," she said.

"Oh no. I need to take my eleven o'clock pills. My alarm just went off to remind me."

"I'll go see if we can get replacements," Eli said, standing up with a groan. "The nurses are going to hate us."

"I'll go with you," Candice said, standing up as well. Even though it was late, she felt restless. She couldn't stop thinking about the house. She loved the farmhouse, and hoped it would be okay.

The three of them ventured out into the hall. It was eerily quiet this late at night. She could hear a door shut somewhere else in the building, but there was no one else in the hall with them.

"Hopefully someone's in," Eli said. "Last time, I had to go to the front office to find someone."

"The medicine pantry is usually still staffed before

midnight," Reggie said, making his slow way down the hall. Candice and Eli followed. Sure enough, when they reached the door that led to the small pharmacy, one of the nurses was there. She took Reggie's name, checked a chart, sighed, then turned to get the correct medication for him. Before handing it over, she picked up a walkie-talkie and called another employee over. They both checked the medication against Reggie's charts and signed a piece of paper, then handed it to him with a glass of water. He made as if to go back to his room with it, but the nurse shook her head.

"I'm sorry, Reggie, but you've gotta take them where we can see it. This policy was put in place because of what happened to you, after all. We can't let anyone scoot around the rules."

"Fine, fine," Reggie said with a sigh. He downed the pills, then the water, and handed the plastic cups back to them. "Satisfied?"

"Very. We'll see you at six for your next round of medication. Try to get some rest."

They walked back down the hall. Candice and Reggie chatted together, wondering what the chef would serve for breakfast, until Eli stopped dead in front of them. Candice peered around him to see what he was looking at, then frowned.

Felix was sitting in the hallway, his tail curled around the front of his paws, looking every bit as comfortable there as if it was his own house.

"What is he doing out?" Eli asked in a whisper.

"I don't know. I swear we locked the door, and I don't think he slipped out without us noticing."

"It looks like the door's open a crack," her husband said.

She and Eli exchanged a look, then he slowly edged forward. Reggie made to follow him, but his grandson shook his head.

"You stay here in the hallway," he said. "Shout if you see someone – anyone at all."

"He's right," Candice told him when it looked like Reggie was about to argue. "If there is someone in there, it could be the person who's after you. And we do need someone watching our backs. I'm going with you, though, Eli."

Together, they inched slowly toward the door. Eli reached forward and pushed it open, and Candice heard a giggle from inside.

"Reggie, is that you?"

She took another step forward and saw Lainey in the middle of the room, holding a picture of Reggie and Eli that she must have picked up off one of the shelves.

"Oh, it's his handsome grandson," she said. "Is Reggie here? I heard one of the nurses say that he was back."

"Word travels fast here," Eli said with a sigh. "He's here, but it's late and we were about to go to bed. He'll see you in the morning, I'm sure."

"Where is he? I'm sure he'd want to see me now. I've got something for him." She gestured at the table, where a familiar looking gift basket was sitting. Candice frowned at it, wondering how on earth Lainey had gotten it.

"You shouldn't even be in here," Eli said, sounding annoyed. "How did you get in? We were sure we locked the door behind us." He took another step into the room, just past the edge of the open door, and Candice screamed as a looming black shape came out from behind the door and wrapped an arm around his neck. Eli struggled, but the man holding on to him was much bigger and stronger than he was. It took Candice a moment to recognize who he was in the dark, but soon enough she realized she had seen him a couple of times before.

"Thanks, Lainey," the man said. He crooked his neck around so he could see Candice over Eli's head. "You, call your grandfather in here, or I'll make sure this young man never walks again."

"Please, don't," Candice said, her eyes tearing up as she watched Eli struggle. The man's fingers were digging into his neck. "Just let him go."

"Get the old man in here!"

"No!" Candice said. It came out as a sob. She knew she was panicking, but there was nothing she could do about it. How could she sacrifice one member of her family for another?

The choice was taken from her when she felt Reggie brush by her. Morgan tossed Eli aside as soon as he spotted him. He grabbed Reggie by the front of his shirt and yanked him closer. She saw him take some-thing out of his pocket – it looked like a hypodermic needle.

"What are you doing?" Lainey asked from behind Morgan.

"I'm silencing the last loose end for good," he snarled. "I'll have to take care of the witnesses too. You'll have to create a distraction while I move the bodies out."

"Bodies?" the old woman asked, her voice quivering. "You said you were just going to threaten them. You promised me no one else would get hurt. You said what happened to Rudy was a... a mistake."

"Just shut up," Morgan snarled. "His death will be quick. A syringe full of air injected in the right spot will look just like a heart attack. No one will know you were involved."

He pressed the needle to Reggie's neck. Candice felt frozen. She was terrified that if she moved even a muscle, he would do it. Out of the corner of her eye, she could see Eli getting up, massaging his throat with one hand. She just needed to stall.

But she didn't have any time to think of a way to do it. She saw Morgan fit his thumb over the syringe's plunger, and knew she had to act. Hoping that she was making the right choice, she lunged for him – but before she even touched him, the man's head jerked back and there was the sound of glass shattering as something hit the floor.

He dropped Reggie, who stumbled but managed to keep to his feet. Candice quickly pulled him out of harm's way. Morgan ignored her. Instead, he turned his head to stare in shock at

Lainey. Candice could see a bleeding cut on the back of his head, and a shattered picture frame on the floor, and realized Lainey had thrown the picture at him.

"That's it," Morgan snarled. "You just lost your last chance. You're not getting your money – you won't even be getting out of here alive."

He had dropped the syringe, but he reached into his coat pocket and Candice saw the glint of something metallic. Before he could fully withdraw whatever weapon he had, he stumbled back, almost tripping over Candice and Reggie, who barely got out of the way. Eli had managed to tackle him around the waist just in time.

Morgan stumbled back and out the door. For a second, it looked like he was about to catch his balance and fight Eli off, but then a calico shape darted between his feet and he tripped, going down hard. Eli didn't hesitate; he hurried back into the room and shut the door hard, locking it.

His breathing was raspy as he met Candice's wide eyes. The room was silent for a moment, until Candice heard the crunch of broken glass behind her. She spun around to see Lainey standing there, tears in her eyes.

"I didn't know he would kill anyone," she whispered. "I swear I didn't."

Something pounded on the door. Eli shot one last, wary look at it, then hurried over to the phone and dialed three digits.

"I don't understand. How did you get involved in all of this? Why did Morgan want to kill Reggie?"

"He offered me money," Lainey said. "Not for me, but for my daughter. She's been struggling so much, and he said all I had to do was help him – sneak into the medicine pantry, open the door when he got here late at night, that sort of thing. It should have been easy. I stole a key to the medicine pantry a long time ago, and everyone knows I have insomnia, so no one would care if I was wandering around at night. He said he just needed my help to get back what should have been his in the first place. He promised he would just threaten people; he wouldn't actually hurt them. I thought Rudy was a mistake. He told me his heart gave out, and he seemed so shaken up by it..." She trailed off, her eyes haunted.

"I don't understand why he was doing all of this in the first place," Candice said as the door rattled again.

"Something about stocks," Lainey said. "He said Rudy stole some stocks from him."

"Stocks," Reggie muttered, slapping the palm of his hand to his forehead. "I thought they were arguing about socks! I heard Morgan and Rudy in the hall, arguing about socks – stocks – Rudy had bought unfairly from Morgan's father. He said he wanted them back, or else. I thought it was just a silly argument, and I told them so! Socks! I'm such an idiot."

"He thought you were a liability, since you'd over-heard and knew he had motive to hurt Rudy." Lainey looked sad. "I still can't believe he killed my Rudy. Maybe it really was an accident; Rudy did have a weak heart, and killing him wouldn't have gotten Morgan what he wanted."

The door shook again as Morgan threw his weight at it. Eli looked up from where he was on the phone. "The police are on their way," he said. "All we have to do is sit tight."

EPILOGUE

CANDICE TIPTOED down to the kitchen, knowing that only one other member of the household would be awake this early. Sure enough, her mother was already in the kitchen, brewing a pot of coffee. She looked up when Candice came in.

"Couldn't sleep?" she asked.

"I'm meeting Emmy for breakfast before work," Candice said. "I think we're going to end up being good friends. I guess that's one good thing that has come out of all of this."

"Well, you'll have a new porch come spring."

Candice gave a quiet chuckle. "Yeah, that too. And new siding. I'm just glad the house is all right."

"I'm glad that the person who did it is behind bars," her mother said, growing more serious. "He tried to kill three people to cover up what he did to Rudy."

"I know. It's scary, how easily he could have killed one or all of us. I guess he really wasn't a killer at heart, though. After all, he admitted that he never meant to kill Rudy."

Morgan had told the police everything once he was in custody. He had tried to kidnap him so he could threaten him into signing over the stocks, but then his heart gave out and he found himself with a dead body instead of wealth in the stock market. Then he panicked and drove out to the loneliest part of the lake that he could find, smashed through the ice, and dumped the body. It was sheer luck that Candice and Eli had found him.

"I'm just glad my family is okay," her mother said. "And I'm including Reggie in that. How is he doing?"

"Great," Candice said, smiling. "He's happy to be back at the nursing home, and has been enjoying being able to talk about his adventures. I think yesterday's the first time he didn't mention what happened at all — he was talking about Eli all day instead."

"Well, his grandson got a small business loan," her mother said. "That's huge."

"I know. I'm so happy for him. For both of us."

Candice couldn't help but grin as her mother poured the coffee. It had been a tough few weeks, but things were finally looking up. Eli had his loan, Reggie was safe and happy, and their house was almost livable again. Pretty soon, things would be back to the way they were before — the same, if not just the slightest bit better, because now Candice had a reminder that it was worth being grateful for the boring times as well as the exciting ones.

ALSO BY PATTI BENNING

Papa Pacelli's Series

Cozy Mystery Tails of Alaska

Book 1: Mushing is Murder

Book 2: Murder Befalls Us

Book 3: Stage Fright and Murder

Book 4: Routine Murder

Book 5: Best Friends and Betrayal

Book 6: Tick Tock and Treachery

Book 7: Lessons and Lethality

AUTHOR'S NOTE

I'd love to hear your thoughts on my books, the storylines, and anything else that you'd like to comment on—reader feedback is very important to me. My contact information, along with some other helpful links, is listed on the next page. If you'd like to be on my list of "folks to contact" with updates, release and sales notifications, etc.... just shoot me an email and let me know. Thanks for reading!

Also...

... if you're looking for more great reads, Summer Prescott Books publishes several popular series by outstanding Cozy Mystery authors.

CONTACT SUMMER PRESCOTT BOOKS PUBLISHING

Twitter: @summerprescott1

Bookbub: https://www.bookbub.com/authors/summer-prescott

Blog   and   Book   Catalog: http://summerprescottbooks.com

Email: summer.prescott.cozies@gmail.com

YouTube: https://www.youtube.com/channel/UCngKNUkDdWuQ5k7-Vkfrp6A

And...be sure to check out the Summer Prescott Cozy Mysteries fan page and Summer Prescott

Books Publishing Page on Facebook – let's be friends!

To download a free book, and sign up for our fun and exciting newsletter, which will give you opportunities to win prizes and swag, enter contests, and be the first to know about New Releases, click here: http://summerprescottbooks.com